BE MORE CHILL

THE GRAPHIC NOVEL

NED VIZZINI

ADAPTED BY
DAVID LEVITHAN

ART BY
NICK BERTOZZI

HYPERION
Los Angeles   New York

First Edition, January 2021
10 9 8 7 6 5 4 3 2 1
FAC-020093-20199
Printed in the United States of America

This book is set in Hedge Backwards, Comicraft/Fontspring
Designed by Marci Senders

Library of Congress Control Number: 2020940948
ISBN (hardcover) 978-1-368-05786-8
ISBN (paperback) 978-1-368-06116-2
Reinforced binding

Visit www.hyperionteens.com

SUSTAINABLE FORESTRY INITIATIVE
Certified Sourcing
www.sfiprogram.org
SFI-00993
Logo Applies to Text Stock Only

1

3

5

11

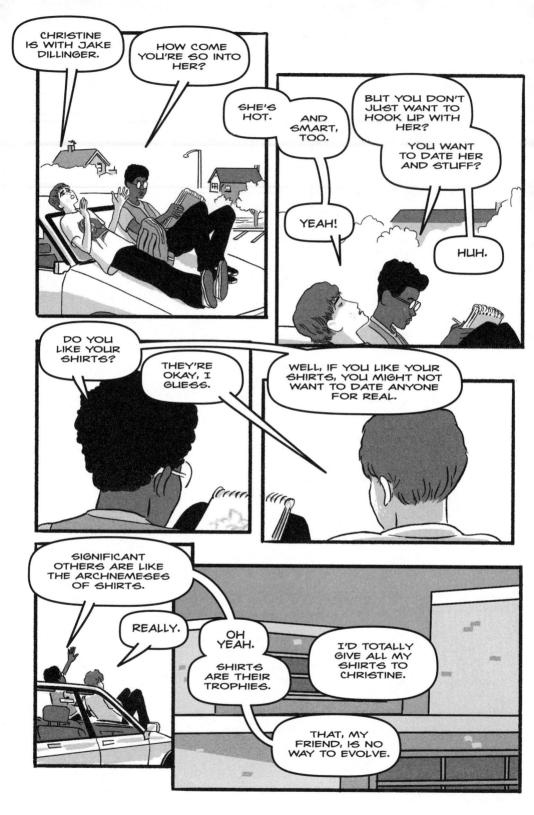

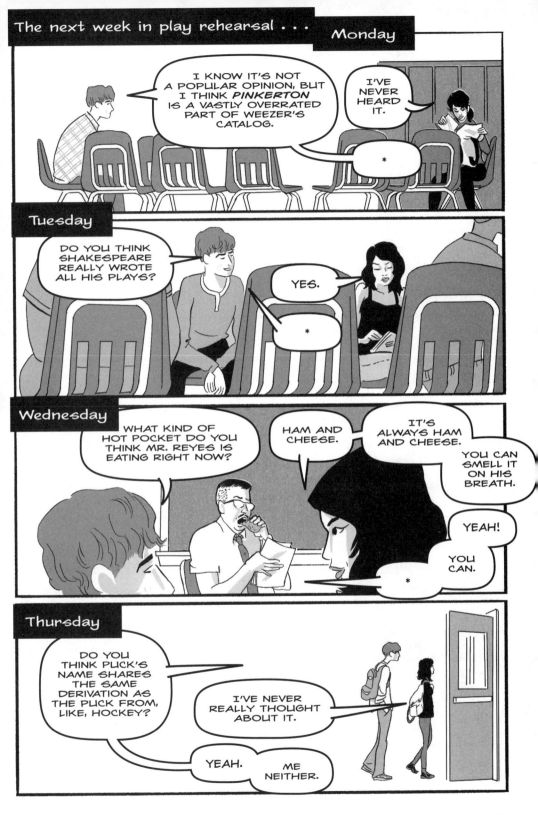

19

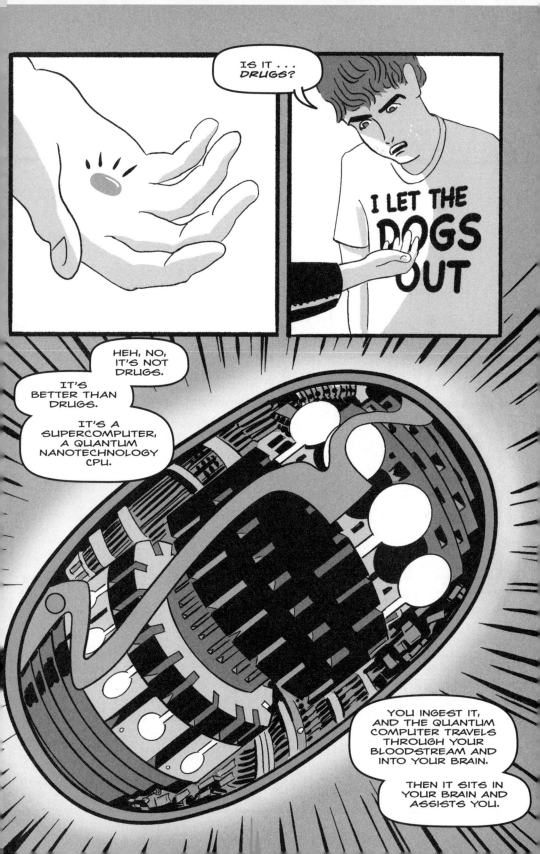

27

30

31

33

39

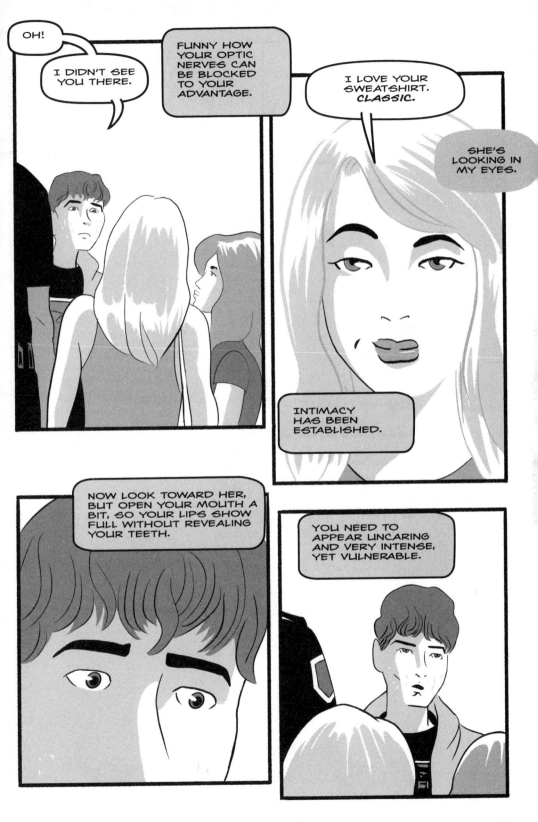

45

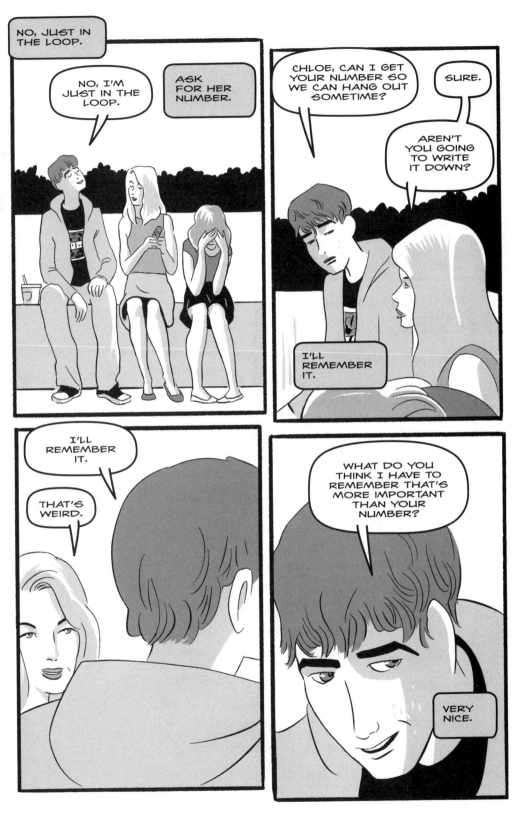

51

NOW LET'S WATCH SOME TV SO I CAN GET MORE INPUT ON THIS UNIVERSE.

EXCELLENT.

THIS WILL HELP ME MAKE DECISIONS ABOUT WHICH TYPES TO TARGET FOR MAXIMUM STATUS.

WELL, I ALREADY KNOW WHICH GIRL I LIKE.

YOU WOULD PREFER TO STAY CONSTRAINED TO YOUR PREFERENCE?

UH, YEAH.

I REALLY DIG THIS GIRL CHRISTINE—

53

54

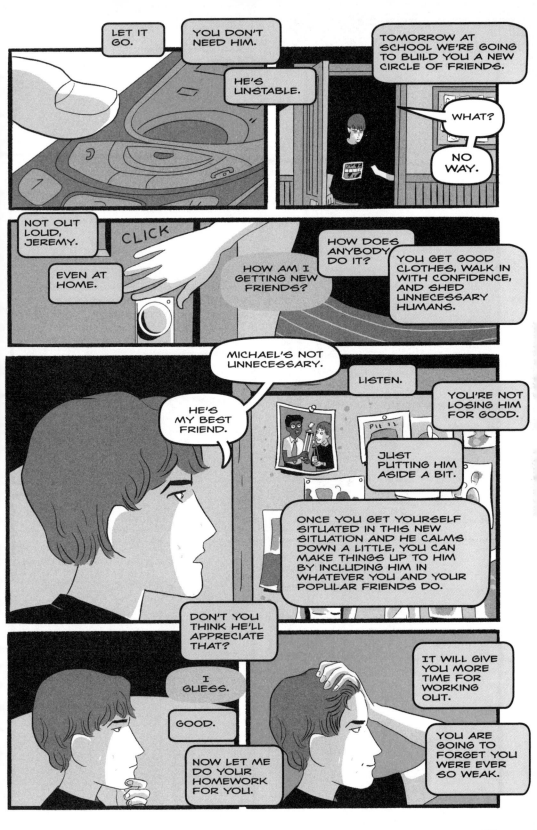

55

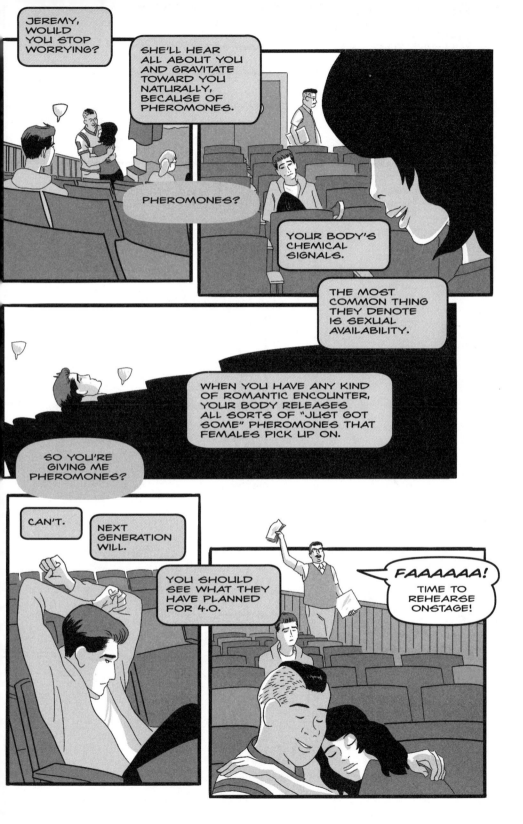

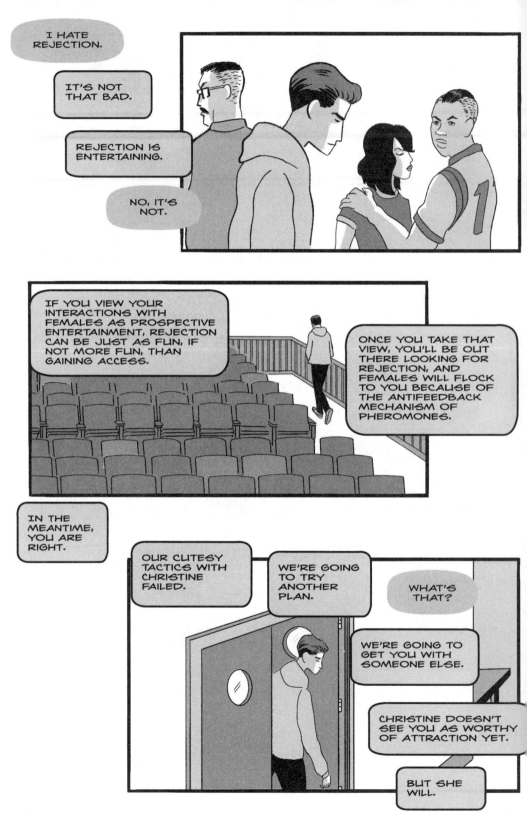

69

01010011110

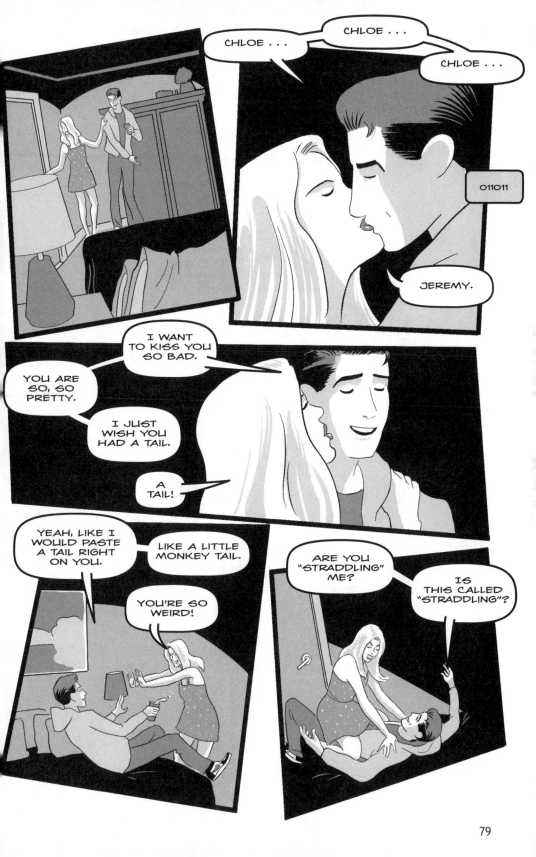

SLAM

DONK

89

95

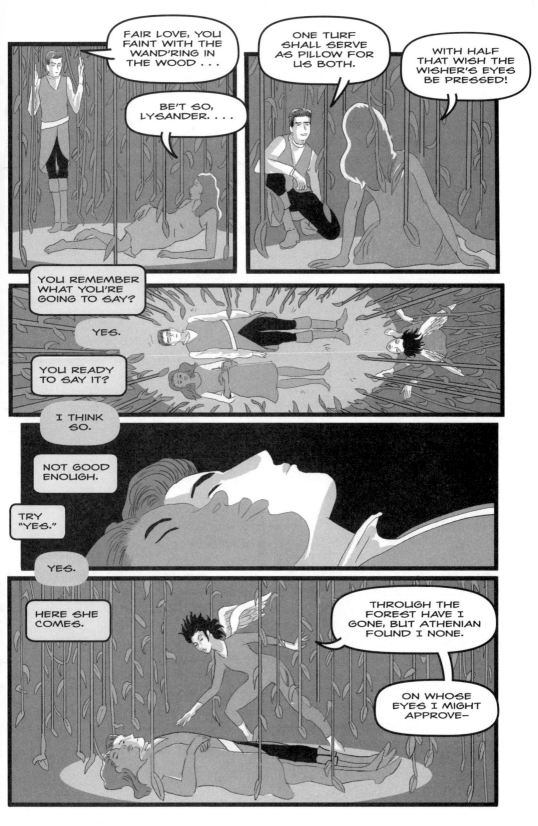

119

120

121

125

129

133

135

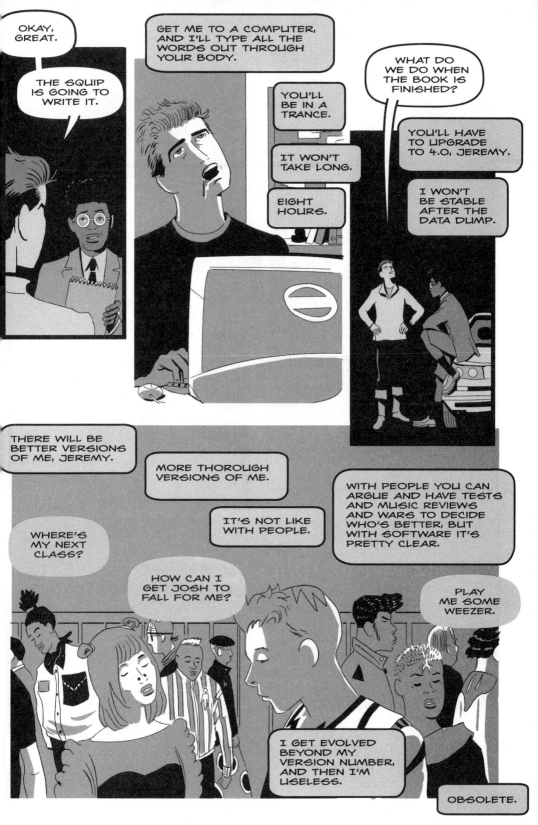

137

I laugh in my head, and then aloud, and then with my friend, and then with the whole night and all of New Jersey and this big stinking silly little planet.

So here you go, Christine. It's not a letter; it's a whole book.

I hope you like it.